Clifford THE BIG RED DOG®
Clifford Helps Santa

by Sonia Sander
Illustrated by Robbin Cuddy

Based on the Scholastic book series
"Clifford The Big Red Dog"
by Norman Bridwell

ISBN 0-439-90456-0

16 15 14 13

11 12 13 14/0

D1005437

SCHOLASTIC INC.

New York   Toronto   London   Auckland   Sydney
Mexico City   New Delhi   Hong Kong   Buenos Aires

Clifford and his friends
were waiting for Christmas.
"I hope Santa gets me
a new ball," said Cleo.

"I want a bowl with
my name on it," said T-Bone.

"I am going to wait up for Santa," said Clifford.

"That is what you said last year.

But then you fell asleep," said Cleo.

Clifford went into his house.

"Good night, Clifford," said Emily
Elizabeth.

It was getting late. Snow was falling.

Clifford waited and waited.

Then, Clifford heard bells.

It was Santa!

Oops!

Santa crashed into the snow.

Woof! Woof!

Clifford ran to help Santa.

He pulled and tugged.

Santa, the reindeer, and the sleigh
came free.

"Good boy, Clifford!" said Santa.

"The reindeer need a rest, Clifford.

Can you give me a ride?" asked Santa.

Santa hopped on Clifford's back.

Soon the snow stopped.
Clifford ran with Santa and his
big bag of toys.

They took gifts to everyone.

They went to the big lighthouse.

They went to the little houses.

"We did it, Clifford," said Santa.

"That was the last gift."

Woof! Woof!

"Good dog, Clifford!" said Santa.

Santa and the reindeer flew off.

"Ho! Ho! Ho!" Santa said.

"Merry Christmas!"

Clifford was very tired.

"I told you he would fall asleep
and miss Santa," said Cleo.

Clifford opened his eyes.

"No, I didn't," he said. "I stayed up and helped Santa."

Just then, Emily
Elizabeth called him.

"See what Santa left,"
Emily Elizabeth said.

"Merry Christmas, Clifford!"

Do You Remember?

Circle the right answer.

What did Santa give Clifford?

1. A bone
2. A collar
3. A ball

Which happened first?

Which happened next?

Which happened last?

Write a 1, 2, or 3 in the space after each sentence.

Clifford got a present from Santa. _____

Santa got stuck in the snow. _____

Clifford and his friends played in the snow. _____

Answers:

Clifford and his friends played in the snow. (1)

Santa got stuck in the snow. (2)

Clifford got a present from Santa. (3)

1. A bone